GHOST VS ALIEN VS EVIL

Kaushik Sathish

Cover design by: Gabriel Mutafchiev

CONTENTS

CHAPTER 1- I'M A GHOST

Hello, my name is Harry. I'm a Ghost. I've been living in this huge building for a very very long time. And this is my story. For years, I've been thinking, or at least the way humans reacted whenever they saw me, had made me think that I'm the scariest and most evil thing on this planet. But one fine day, I realized I'm not even close to that.

Huge building

This building was my only home forever, as those who brought me into existence has also made sure that I cannot even move an inch out of this building. Let me give you a brief history of my sweet home. The building is pretty ancient. Its been here even before I came into existence. The building was initially a sacred structure built by ancient humans. Then some King saw how huge it was and decided to turn it into his palace. Then the King's son ruled for a few years, and then he died. So his son ruled for some decades, and finally, his son, who was a daughter, but was forced to act as a boy so that she could continue the dynasty, ruled for few years. Only around this time, I came into existence.

The daughter was the last of the dynasty as she brought the kingdom down with a little help from me. After that, a few more kings tried to live in the place, but then they didn't stay there for too long due to my presence and the place's negative history.

After that, I've been lonely for many long decades. There was no

TV, Radio or any entertainment for me to have fun. Above all, there weren't any human beings who were the main source for my mind peace. Scaring them was my only purpose. It was the only reason for which I came into existence.

A few more decades passed and some people started entering the palace now and then. But unfortunately, they were dead inside to be scared by me. No matter how hard I tried to gain their attention, they were too busy fighting with each other. They wore specific suits and were armed with weapons and they simply killed each other. Yes, they were soldiers fighting the world war. No matter how much I tried to scare them, they didn't seem to mind me that much. During their fights, they also destroyed my beautiful home. After this, several more lonely decades passed. Finally, one fine day, 5 people entered the place. My instincts were killing me from inside and every part of me wanted to scare the hell out of them. But, I controlled myself.

I've learned that if I scare them too soon, they will run away leaving me alone again. So I hid, spied, and stalked them. This group of people was very different from the people that I've been seeing all these years. They are the reason I came to know about the different technological devices like Television etc.. These people started making many adjustments to my home and they made it look different from what it was. Now, my home was looking good and new, but I kind of hated it. Because now, my home was full of light no matter if the sun is up or not. It is now difficult for me to stay hidden. I have to find specific places to hide and often had to stay there for a very long time. Eventually, a few months after my home was modified, a new family moved in and started to live there. Finally, I was back on my business.

Good times

The new family consisted of 5 people. 2 adults and 2 teenagers and a 5-year-old girl. I managed to control my instincts for a few days. All those days, I was trying to have fun with the 5-year-old girl because for some reason the adults don't believe if their little ones claim that hey saw me. But no matter how hard I tried, I ended up getting a different experience from the girl. They called her Suki. A few weeks passed, and I slowly started to get my hands on the teenagers. Those were good times for me. Scaring the hell out of those creatures who were occupied to their phones always. Most of the time, when I tried to get gain their attention, I end up failing due to those phones in their hands. So, usually, I had to wait until late at night when they keep their damn phones and try to go to sleep. So during the day times, I hid and watched television along with the adults or listen to music whenever they played them.

Now, coming to the different experiences that I had with Suki. Whenever I get her attention to scare her, I saw a different reaction on her eyes. She wasn't scared of me for some reason. There were times when I worried that I wasn't scary anymore. But the teenagers proved me wrong. She introduced me to a different concept which the humans called "Friendship". But before I talk about my first friend, let me give you a brief introduction to how I came into existence.

My Birth

So, remember the daughter who was forced to be a boy so that she could continue the dynasty? Yes, she was named Sukran. She is the reason I exist in this world. Before that, all I could remember was total darkness. I wasn't able to move anywhere or do anything. All I could do is to stare into the darkness.

One fine day, I saw a light above me. It was like a door opened above me. Through that door, I could hear a sweet was calling out for me. Her voice just dragged me from the darkness through the door like opening, and to this world. The first human face I saw was her's. Since this is the first time I'm entering this strange world and seeing a human, I didn't know how to react. And probably, it was the first time she saw someone like me. So, she was pretty scared of me. She immediately ran out of the room leaving me alone. I was confused and was roaming here and there in her room. I stumbled and pushed down a few of her furniture. After a while, I got tired and went to a dark corner and rested for a while.

After a few minutes, Sukran entered the room with an elderly woman with a staff on her hand and long white hair. She was called the Witch. I could sense that she was scared of me. But, for some reason, she pretended not to be scared. The Witch did some magic after which I was able to understand human language. She started commanding me with a deep voice. She clearly explained who I am and what was my purpose. My purpose was to help Sukran scare people. Sukran wanted me to be her ally and portray her as a girl with evil powers. Since I didn't have anything in my life a few minutes before, I agreed to whatever she said. I was like their baby. But a really scary one. The Witch gave me some rules. I must obey Sukran. I must show myself only when Sukran asks to do so and I must do whatever Sukran asks me to do. And finally, the Witch finished her job with me and left.

CHAPTER 2- REBELLION

It took a while before I and Sukran connected. She was a very timid girl but was forced every time by her parents and ministers to act boldly in front of the people. She was forced to dress, act, talk, and walk like a boy every time. There was a lot of time when she enters her room, threw herself on her bed, and cried. I always wanted to console her and be with her. But she never asked for my help. She commanded me to be in a dark corner of her room until she wants to see me again. So I obeyed.

Time to time, her eyes glance towards my corner, but she quickly turns away. Whenever her eyes looked at my direction, a sense of excitement arouse in me. But it faded immediately as she never bothered me. A lot of days passed since my birth into this strange world. But I still felt as if I was back in the dark again. One fine day, she behaved differently. She entered her room and cried a lot than usual. Then she stopped crying and kept on staring towards me for a while. Her face became pale and dull due to all those crying. I was thinking that finally, she wants to see me again. But she just stared for a very long while, then she went out of her room. She returned with a glass inside which there was some beverage.

Once again, she sat on her bed, stared at me, and at that glass of beverage. After a while, she took the glass on her hand and was about to drink it. But she couldn't. So she kept it back and again stared at me. She was repeating these actions for a while until finally, she seemed to have made a decision. She picked up the glass and decided to drink it. Suddenly, someone called her from outside. She kept the glass down with her shaky hands and went out of the room. I couldn't control my curiosity to see what was inside that glass that scared her so much. So, I decided to break my orders and take a quick peek inside the glass before she returned.

I moved out of my dark corner quickly towards the glass. I reached where the glass was and this was the first time I realized that I cannot face the light. A ray of sunlight passed through the curtain of her window and shined on me when I was near the glass. I felt a sharp burning sensation all over my body.
I quickly tried to move away from the light. When I did that, I tumbled on the furniture on which the glass was placed. I managed to quickly return to where I was. But the sound of the glass hitting the ground gained Sukran's attention. She slowly entered the room and immediately noticed the glass with the beverage spilled on the ground. Suddenly, she realized that I must have been the one who made this mess as there wasn't anyone else in the room.

She walked towards me with some hesitation. She looked at me sometimes and finally, she asked me to come out of my corner and face her. I obeyed. Initially, I could sense terror on her face when she saw me. But she came over it quickly. She clearly explained the misery she is been going through from her birth. And the beverage which I accidentally spilled was her way to end them. Since that's out of the way, now she decided to go with her plan B, which included me.

The Final Show

She created a clever and pretty bold plan. In the next two days, her father, the King, planned a big ceremony after which Sukran will rule the land as the King. But Sukran clearly couldn't handle such stress. So, she asked me to help her out by acting as an entity, which came into existence due to the turmoils she had to go through. She wanted to create fear amongst everyone. I was nervous about how I would scare such a huge number of people. By then, I didn't know that I looked very scary for humans.

So as planned, the ceremony began grandly, and the time came when the King announced to the public about the next ruler. Sukran came to the stage where her father was waiting with a crown on his hand. When her father tried to place the crown on her head, she pushed the crown away and removed all her make up and dressing which made her appear like a man. She revealed herself as a woman. The angry king commanded the guards to arrest her. According to the plan, I must show myself only when she calls me. But Sukran was so scared that she forgot about me. But I saw the arrogant guards running towards her and I saw her face which was losing all hopes. So, I couldn't control my instincts. I jumped in front of her and revealed myself. The way the rude soldiers came to her made me angry. That's when I realized how scary I was to these humans.

One of the soldiers fell unconscious immediately and the others were pale and speechless. The King couldn't believe what he saw. Sukran quickly joined and everything went as per the plan. With the help of some magical effects provided by the witch, Sukran could convey a clear message that no woman should ever go through what she has been through. Making a women do so, will unleash the darkness within her and the entire land will be haunted by the darkness thereafter.

My presence and her message stopped the King's heart from working. Chaos burst out in the kingdom and some soldiers tried to harm me with their weapons. But they couldn't I was incorporeal. The only thing that could harm me was light and I was clever enough to evade those places filled with light. See, back then there were abundant dark places due to the lack of electricity. I kept on scaring away anyone who tried to get close to Sukran while she managed to escape to her room. People were running everywhere screaming for their life. I had some fun for a while.

But after the palace became empty, I didn't know what to do anymore. So, I decided to go back to Sukran's room.

As I entered her room, I saw her with a bag full of her things and she was standing near her window. She turned back and looked at me. I smiled at her with great joy. I wanted to dance and celebrate with her for successfully executing our plan and ending her misery. But she didn't smile back at me. I could sense a little happiness on her face. But it started to get dimmer the longer she stared at me. The happiness changed into a bit of fear. But despite her fear, I could sense that she wanted to convey something to me as if she wanted to thank me for my help. But suddenly, there was a voice calling her down from out the window asking her to hurry up. So, she threw her bag out and climbed out of the window leaving me alone.

I wished that I could follow her because without her I didn't know what else to do. She was like my mother. But it was midday and the sun was at its maximum brightness. Still, I couldn't resist so I ran near the window only to get severely burnt by the sun. Through the pain, I tried to see where she was. She was sitting behind a man on a horse and was riding far away. She was looking towards the window up until a point when she turned her head. Then we never saw each other again.

CHAPTER 3- LONELY DAYS ARE GONE

Her act left me desperate. I felt a great sense of anger towards every human. So, I started to scare the hell out of every human I met afterward. There were these particular humans who dressed strangely and brought some holy water and stuff to chase me away. Though some of that stuff caused me immense harm, my rage was so high that they couldn't handle my terror. They usually flee away after putting some magic that restricts me from being in a particular area of the palace. But they fade away after a long time and I can again roam anywhere freely.

Then slowly, people started to stop visiting the palace. Then begun my lonely days, roaming here and there around the palace. Several times after the sun was down, I've tried to go away from the castle. But whenever I take a step away from the castle's interior and try to go to the outside world, I immediately get thrown back inside. That's when I realized that I was created in such a way that I could only exist inside the castle. All those days, I could only think about Sukran. But as time passed and new events happened in the castle, I slowly started to forget about her and my rage towards humans cooled down. As I told before, several people visited, and finally, I ended up with this family.

Old feeling

As I told before, my encounter with Suki was different. Since she was just a kid, she remembered me of my old days when I first came into existence and didn't know what to do. I could relate so much to Suki. So, I didn't want to scare her immediately. Something was stopping me from scaring her, though I had a lot of great opportunities in which I could have easily scared her while still maintaining my cover. I calmly watched her hiding in the dark. But the longer.

But as days passed, my urge to have some fun was rising inside me. So, I tried my tricks on the teenagers and it worked well. I calmed myself by playing with the teenagers now and then. One day I decided that it is about time to interact with the little one, as too much interaction with the teenagers might cause some suspicion amongst the adults. So, I decided to pause having fun with them and try the little one. But instead of scaring her, I tried a different approach. I decided to just appear in front of her for a moment, and disappear, just so that I could see how she reacted. I did as I planned.

Shame

But to my surprise, her reaction was different from what I expected. The kid smiled at me as soon as she saw me. Her smile, to be honest, scared the hell out of me. Because since my birth, all I saw was fear on the face of every human whenever they saw me. This is the first time a human being smiled at me. The sudden change in the usual caused me immense fear. So, I ran away and disappeared.

I went to a dark corner, relaxed, and turned back only to get more scared as the little one was searching for me. Her eyes got locked onto the dark corner in which I was hiding. The girl slowly walked towards me. The closer she got, the scarier it was for me. I was strongly hoping that the darkness wouldn't reveal me. Thankfully, when she was at a reasonable distance, her mother called her to eat. She went away leaving me to relax. From that night, I didn't want to scare anyone in the family, as I was so preoccupied by my encounter with the little one. For the next two days, it was clear that she was searching for me. But I hid from her.

Finally, one fine day, I decided that this wasn't right for me. I could spend all my time thinking and hiding from the little one, or I could do something about it. I reminded myself of whom I was and how I used to terrorize the humans. So, I planned to scare the little one without showing any mercy. I waited until it was dark. I could see her tiny body sleeping on the bed. I slowly crawled and reached her. As I got close to her, my fear started building up. But I cheered myself up. After all, what could her little body do to me that all those strangely dressed people with holy water and stuff couldn't? I told myself.

I climbed over her bed without making any noise and by making as few moves as possible. I put my face a few inches above her face and stared at her with my big round red-colored eyes, waiting for her to open her eyes so that I could unleash the terror. After a few minutes, she opened her tiny but beautiful eyes slowly. I quickly opened my big mouth to show the thousands of crisscrossed sharp teeth of mine.

What happened next was a huge disappointment to me. The little one glanced at me for a few seconds and went back to sleep. I felt a great sense of shame. All these waiting and stalking just for this? I kept asking myself. I also excused myself by giving reasons such as The kid must have been too tired to react, or it was too dark that she couldn't see me properly, etc.. But I also realized that I have scared people even at times when they were about to die and only during the dark I appear scarier. I was too confused. I tried waiting there for a few more minutes, but the kid seemed to be deep asleep. So, I didn't feel like trying anymore. I left with a great sense of failure and shame.

I'm nothing

I waited patiently for the sun to peek a bit so that there was enough darkness for me to not get affected by the sunlight and enough light for the girl to see me. It was dawn. I slowly entered the kid's room. I got behind her bed as stealthily as possible. Then

I pushed one of her toys so that it made a subtle noise which was enough to wake the kid up.

The kid opened her eyes and simply stared at the ceiling. I could see in her eyes that sleep hasn't still left her completely. I waited for her to turn and look at where the noise came from so that I could make a surprising jump in front of her and scare her. It was about time, I widened my blood-like eyes and kept my mouth ready to be open. But instead of looking down to her side, from where the noise came from, she directly looked back where I was standing. She caught me all of sudden and I didn't know how to react. I was standing there like a dumb ass. When she saw me, she started smiling at me again. Fear started to build inside my body. Every instinct told me to run away and hide immediately. But I controlled them and tried to put my best show. I widened my eyes again and opened my mouth as much as possible exposing all of my razor-sharp looking teeth. I even moved towards her a little bit as if I'm going to attack her.

But she kept on smiling at me. Fear took control of my body gain as she got up out of her bed and tried to walk towards me. She put her hands up towards me as if she wanted me to pick her up. I backed off as much as possible until I hit a wall. When I hit the wall, I accidentally pushed a photo frame that was hanging on the wall. The photo fell to the ground and shattered into pieces creating a huge noise that got the attention of Suki's mother. I didn't know what to do. If I leave the room, chances are that her mother could spot me. So, I looked around the room and the only hiding spot I could find was under Suki's bed. I quickly moved and hid under her bed. I could hear her mom rushing towards the room screaming Suki's name.

I thought this was it for my time with this family. My lonely days are about to begin again. I could imagine Suki pointing under her bed when her mother asks her how the photo was broken. Because obviously, Suki isn't tall enough to do that, neither was there any wind flow in the room. Her mom entered the room and I could hear her inquiring Suki. They discussed something for a few minutes and the voice of her mother couldn't be heard anymore. I could only see Suki's tiny legs walking towards the bed. I didn't know what to do. I planned to escape quickly, but a bright ray of sunlight entered through her window and fell directly in front of her bed. So, I cannot escape quickly without gaining more attention or hurting myself. Her legs stopped when it reached the bed. I was waiting for her to peek under the bed. But, those legs climbed over the bed.

It was confusing to me. Her mother should have put her face in front of me by now and screamed the hell out of her. But she didn't. Which means Suki hasn't blamed me for the accident. And now she didn't even bother to check on me and went back to the bed? How was this possible? When I was wondering what the hell just happened, few strands of hair peeked from above the bed, followed by the little one's tiny head. She checked on me with the same smile. But this time, it wasn't that scary as it used to be. She slowly reached her tiny arms and tried to touch me. I moved away to the corner, but she still reached her hands towards me and waited patiently for me to respond. So, I slowly extended my hands and tried to touch her hand. But obviously, her hand passed right through my hand as if there was nothing there.

I tired a few times to grab and even she tried her best. But it wasn't possible. After a while, the little one gave up and went away from her room. That incident made me realize that I'm nothing. I'm something, only if the human mind is open enough to see me and get scared of me. That's why no matter how much I tried to scare the World war soldiers, they didn't seem to mind.

CHAPTER 4-
BLIND ANGER

I just laid under the bed wondering what is the purpose of my existence. All these days I was thinking that my only purpose was to scare every human being. But just now, I realized that my ability to scare humans depends on their minds. Without their minds I'm nothing. Humans have various things to do in their life before they go out of their bodies. Amongst them, the two things I couldn't comprehend was love and compassion. But thanks to Suki I could slowly learn and feel what they meant.

After some long minutes of me, alone under Suki's bed, thinking about my existence, I could see the tiny legs running towards the bed again. This time, instead of fear, there was only curiosity in me. I was wondering what she was going to do now. She peeked under the bed with a small piece of stick in her hand. She reached the stick towards me. I couldn't understand why. But I went along and grabbed the stick. The smile on her face brightened as if she figured out something. She pulled the stick towards her which dragged my hand towards her. That's when I realized how smart the little one was. She contacted me by using the stick as a medium. All those objects that I pushed and interacted with starting from Sukran's beverage glass to the photo came to my mind.

Yes, I could touch and feel objects. I told to myself. She tried to drag me out of under her bed as if I was stuck under there. So, I also tried to come out. But, I completely forgot about the sun rays. I remembered about the rays only after a small portion of my fingers got burned by the rays. As a reflex, I quickly retracted my hands back. My quick action made Suki realize immediately that something was wrong. But she couldn't understand what was wrong. She was looking at the stick. So, I tried to explain it to her by miming. I pointed towards the sun rays and shook my head negatively.

The little one quickly stood up and went towards the window, closed it, and dragged her curtain, which covered the sunlight and created enough darkness for me to get out.

Best days of my life

I crawled out from under the bed and stood in front of her. The fear inside me was replaced immediately with a new feeling which I've experienced for the very first time in my life. She again took that piece of stick and reached towards me. But I had another idea. There was a cotton doll amongst the group of toys that was in her room. I went and picked up the doll and used it as a medium to communicate with her. She also appreciated the idea and thus our Friendship begun.

We spent a lot of time together. I watched Television with her, listened to songs, watch her draw. She even made a lot of sketches of me and made me look good than how I looked. We shared many moments. The moments I could never forget. Under her bed was my new home. She kept the medium doll always under her bed. Usually, she calls her mom in the midnight to accompany her in case she wanted to use the toilet. But now, it was my job to accompany her. I didn't feel like scaring away people anymore. All I wanted was to spend time with my little friend. That was enough for me.

The bully guy

 Several months of these happy days continued. Suki started to spend a lot of time with me. Every day as soon as she returned home from school, she runs straight to her room to greet me. And I also eagerly waited every day for her return home. As soon as she meets me, the first thing she does is to narrate her day at the school. She liked everything about the school, except for a guy named Johnson. He always creates trouble with her by taking away her things or her lunch. Only if I could get out of this house, I could scare the hell out of him and keep him away from my little one. But obviously, I couldn't.

One fine day she came home crying. As soon as I heard her crying voice, I couldn't standstill. I wanted to know what happened to her. So, I peeked out of her room and tried to listen to what happened to her as her mother was inquiring about what happened to her. But, she refused to explain anything to her mother and just wanted to get inside her room to meet me. But her parents seemed to be worried about her and didn't let her go without getting an explanation of what happened. But the actions of her parents made her only cry more. So, they decide to leave her alone.

She came inside her room and hugged the doll which we used as a medium and cried for a few minutes. I tried to console her by using the doll and tried to make a funny dance to make her happy. I worked! She finally stopped crying and laughed a bit seeing me dance funnily. You know what? In all these years of scaring away these humans, I used several skills and tricks to scare them as much as possible. Every time, I tried to be much scarier than before. But none of those gave me a sense of great achievement and satisfaction as her laugh gave me when I did something which was out of my area of expertise. I was very proud of myself that day.

After she calmed down a bit, she started to explain to me what was that which made her cry. As I suspected, it was Johnson. Not only he stole her favorite pencil, but he also threw water on her pants and complained that she peed on herself. That action gave Suki a great sense of shame as everyone in her class laughed at her. That's the reason why she was very upset. Her upset woke my hidden hatred towards human beings. All I wanted at that moment was to be in front of Johnson and unleash my terror. But I cannot. So, I and Suki came with a plan. I asked Suki to draw the most terrifying version of me and asked her to show it to Johnson. And I asked Suki to warn Johnson saying that I'm her friend and if he doesn't stop messing with her I will visit him every night.

My stupid plan

Suki agreed and did as I asked. What the hell did I think? Me and my stupid plan. Turns out, when Suki did as asked, Johnson laughed at her much more, grabbed the picture of me, and showed it to the teachers. The teachers were worried about Suki's behavior and they ended up talking with their parents about this. From that day onwards, Suki's parents were deeply worried about her mental health for some reason. Her mother regularly checked what she was doing alone in her room and I had to hide often. I hated this. I wanted my good old peaceful times with Suki back. And I'm pretty sure Suki hated this too. I was upset that I was the primary reason for all these stupid events. But Suki always consoled me saying it wasn't my fault.

The more her parents started bothering her, the more Suki wanted to spend time alone with me. Everyone at her school started her to look differently and now even her family members looked at her differently. I was the only true friend she had who loved her for what she was. So, she wanted to spend more time with me rather than spending time with other humans. There were times at which even I compelled her to go outside and mingle with other humans, as I knew that was good for her. Though on the one hand, I was happy that I got a friend like Suki, on the other hand, I was worrying that I might become a disturbance in her life. And I didn't want myself to be a reason for her life being destroyed.

CHAPTER 5- END OF GOOD TIMES

One fine day, Suki's teenage sister who usually never bothers to interact with her much, decided to check on her. As usual, I hid under the bed and was listening to their conversation. She was explaining all teenage nonsense such as, how Suki would never get a boyfriend if she always stayed in her room like this and other stupid teenage stuff.

But Suki never minded whatever she said. She started to go around Suki's room and check her things. She ended up finding some of Suki's drawings of me and she seemed to recognize me from my previous encounter with her. She screamed the hell out of her and immediately ran to her mom and claimed that something evil is existing in this house and claimed that even she has seen it.

Until this day, their parents were thinking that the drawings were Suki's imagination. But after what her sister said, they started doubting. They came inside Suki's room and constantly questioned her about whether she knew someone or saw someone like me. Suki kept on denying. For the next two nights, they made Suki sleep with them in their room, despite her not wanting to do so. I have spent all these years lonely, but, those two days were much worse compared to all those lonely years. All I could do is see was Suki passing along with her mother to the toilet. Every time she passed she gave a quick smile looking at me. That calmed me for a while. Then finally after a long argument, they let her sleep in her room back again.

For a few days, everything seemed to be going as usual. Just when I and Suki thought that our happy days have returned, everything started to fall apart. Her mom suddenly entered Suki's room with a vacuum cleaner. She said she is about to clean her room as it's been a while since it has been cleaned. Suki tried her best to make her mom clean the room afterward. The more Suki tried to change her mind, the more her mom had a suspicion. So, her mom decided to clean the room immediately no matter what Suki said. She made Suki go out and started cleaning the room. From under the bed, all I could see was her legs moving here and there around, along with the vacuum cleaner. I hoped very much that she didn't have to clean under the bed. I could see Suki peeking from outside the room without knowing what to do.

The moment came, her mom was about to clean under the bed. She came near the bed and started hoovering under the edges of the bed until a point in which the cleaner couldn't reach under the bed anymore unless she bent down. Suddenly, the doorbell rang. She got up and went outside to check who it was. Suki quickly entered the room and closed the curtains so that I could get out and hide somewhere. I immediately got out and hid inside her closet. I knew that her mother wouldn't bother to check in there as she already finished cleaning it. I hid myself successfully and Suki managed to get out of the room before her mother came back.

Apparently, Suki was the one who rang the doorbell, hid herself, and made her way to the room stealthily to help me hide. I was very proud of how she executed the plan. It reminded me of Sukran. Her mother returned to the room wondering who rang the doorbell as there wasn't anybody outside. When asked, Suki was clever enough to say that she didn't hear any doorbell ringing. So, her mom thought that it was probably her imagination, and started cleaning under the bed. I was watching what was happening through the gap between the closet doors. Everything went well except for one thing. After she finished cleaning under the bed, she stood up and seemed confused about something. And then, she realized that the room was dark and the curtain was closed. She called Suki and inquired about this. But Suki lied that she never entered the room. This created fear inside her mother.

Rough night

That night they made Suki to sleep again with them. The next morning Suki was home as it was weekend. She entered the room and we started our daily routine of communicating and playing. Suddenly, we both heard someone entering the house. Both Suki's parents and the teenagers were having a conversation with the stranger. After a few minutes of conversation, I heard them walking towards Suki's room. So, I quickly went and hid inside her closet.

I could hear a man's voice asking Suki's parents to take her away from the room and he closed the door. He was taking a good look around the room. When I saw the man, I could immediately recognize that he was one of those strangely dressed men with holy water and stuff. Suki's parents must have become more suspicious of my presence and must have called him. Now, all I got to do is to hide well and hope he doesn't see me. He waited in front of the closet for a moment and was thinking something. He looked as if he knew that I was inside. I thought he was about to burst open the closet doors and throw something over me which could hurt the hell out of me. But, to my surprise, he just walked away calmly.

My bad

I thought the man didn't know that I was there and that everything is going to be okay. But, unfortunately, he knew that I was present and he asked the family to move out of the house, as he told them that I could be too dangerous for the kids, especially for Suki. From that moment, her parents asked Suki never to enter her room and they were planning to move the next day to their grandparent's house until they find a new home. This made Suki anxious. She didn't want to leave me. I was the only true friend she had. So, she cried and fought her best to convince her parents to not leave the house. She even tried to explain that I'm her friend and I don't mean harm to anyone in any way. But all those explanations caused an opposite effect on their parents and made them want to leave the home as soon as possible.

She cried and cried and all I could hear was her voice calling out my name. "Harry, Harry" she cried. Yes, she is the one who named me Harry. All of that screaming from her little body couldn't help me stay still. I wanted to go out there and hug her. And that's exactly what I tried to do. Maybe if I reveal myself and proved to them that I'm not harmful, they might let Suki to be with me. So, I went out of my hiding and finally appeared in front of their family. There was a huge moment of silence amongst them. Suki gave a huge smile and told, "Look mommy he doesn't want to hurt". But they weren't like Suki. They were like every other human. They were scared to hell and screamed the crap out of them. I couldn't do anything but just stand there and watch them scream at me.

The teenagers ran out of the house screaming, her mother held Suki as tight as possible, her dad was calling the strangely dressed man, who just left, to come back. Suki was trying her best to tell her parents to calm down. I took a few steps closer to show them I wasn't trying to do anything. But the closer I got, the scarier they got. Suddenly, Suki asked me to do the funny dance. I thought that was a great idea. It made Suki laugh, so I could do the same to their parents. Hence, I danced. Turns out, my dancing was much scarier for them than anything else. His father was almost about to faint.

Suddenly, the strangely dressed man busted inside with a book, some holy water, and some other usual stuffs he brings to harm me. His presence angered me. It's all because of him. I thought to myself. So, I opened my mouth exposing my teeth and just went towards him trying to harm him. But he threw some stuff at me which threw me a few feet back. He asked them to get out of the house immediately. Suki screamed and cried. I, on the other hand, wasn't able to move for some reason. Her father took his car keys and ran out asking her mother to bring Suki outside. The strange guy was reading something out of his book. Her mother had to drag Suki out of the house. When Suki was almost near the exit, she managed to free herself from her mother's grip and she ran towards me as quickly as possible. Seeing this the strangely dressed man stopped whatever he was doing and ran behind Suki to grab her.

Suki managed to get close to me and she reached her hand, even I reached mine and tired to grab hers. But guess what happened? Yes. Her hands went right through mine and she ended up falling and hurting herself. The strange guy grabbed her hand and took her outside. I used this moment to quickly escape from there and hide in the attic. That was the end of good times with my first friend.

CHAPTER 6-
HELLO THERE!

I stayed in the attic. Few minutes after all the disaster that happened, I could hear the strange man's voice along with three other human voices chanting some strange stuff and asking me to go away. I stayed calm and didn't appear before them. Though one part of me wanted to get down and wanted to scare them to death after what they did to me, another part of me didn't want to do anything, as deep inside, I knew that I was the reason for all this to happen. But how ironic? All the days when I tried to scare the family, nothing happened. But after I tried to be good with them, everything fell apart.

The strange men did their thing and went away. Since I already had experiences with such guys, I knew that if I tried to get out of the attic and roam, their magic will keep on hurting me. I have to wait for a long time for the magic to fade so that I can roam back again wherever I want around the home. So, I had to stay in the attic for a very long time alone. I didn't have something to do anyway, neither did I want to do something. All I could do is sit there stare at the wall and think about all that happened and all those wonderful days with my only friend. I was just like those teenagers except, instead of staring at the phone, I stared at the wall.

Several months passed, and I didn't move an inch from where I was. One fine day I could hear some human voices. I tried to listen to what they were saying as much as possible. They were people who were trying to sell the house to somebody else. They were talking about me, and they also talked about how I could be only just an imagination by Suki's family and not something real. I knew that those people will somehow manage to sell the house to somebody as soon as possible. Because its a fact that my house is very huge and beautiful. And humans always want such a house.

Those people left and after that, I couldn't see any human activity for a long time. After a while, I had a feeling that the strange men's magic has gone away. My guess wasn't wrong and the magic has indeed faded away.

An old friend

As usual, I was roaming the house in the darkness. I didn't want to enter Suki's room as I was sure it will bring me back all the memories. So, whenever I passed that area, I tried to avoid looking towards the room. But I couldn't control my urge to go and look inside the room for so long. What if Suki somehow escaped from her parents and came to her room searching for me? If I wasn't there won't she be disappointed? Stupid thoughts were fueling my urge to enter the room.

So, I decided to enter the room. But it was completely different. No bed, no toys, and above all, no Suki. I felt a huge pain in me. I hated who I was. Why Sukran had to bring me to this world? Why would I be created in such a way that everyone must hate me? Why should I go through all these sufferings without an ending to it all? I kept asking myself. So, I decided to enter inside the closet and pretend as if everyone was outside and I was just hiding from them. I expected the closet to be empty. But to my surprise, there was something which I didn't expect.

It was the doll that Suki used as a medium to communicate with me. I was extremely happy to see that doll. Suki must have left it for me. I kept saying to myself. I hugged that doll and always stayed with it. The doll was my new companion. I took it everywhere I went. I tried to communicate with it. But of course, it has no life, like Suki. But something was better than nothing.

Some movement again

Some humans entered the home again. They cleaned and painted the house and made it new as before. I knew that someone is probably going to come to the house. What if I could make a new friend? I was excited. So, another few days passed with the doll, as I waited for someone to move. And finally, a family did move to the house.

This time it was only four members. Two adults and two children. A boy and a girl. Both the children were older than Suki but younger than the teenagers. Now I have some hope. What if I could be friends with the kids? If Suki can accept me, surely they can too! I thought. So, I waited for many days before I tried to contact them. I just watched them. They seemed to be normal kids just like Suki. And the parents were the same as Suki's parents. The only small difference is that, both the kids slept in the same room.

One night, I waited until their parents went to sleep and for the kids to sleep as well. I entered the room along with the doll and waited till dawn so that I could try and communicate with them. Dawn came along with a little light enough for the kids to see clearly. I decided to try with the little girl. So, I used the doll to touch and caress her face. The girl woke up from her sleep and saw the doll. She grabbed the doll's hand and seemed to wonder where that came from. She looked back and saw me. I gave a smile. She kept silent and stared at me for a few seconds. And suddenly her expression changed. Her face became pale, her eyes got bigger, her heart pumped faster, and she started to scream. Her scream woke up the boy. Even the boy started screaming when he saw me. I tried to do my funny dance to try and make them laugh. But, it turns out that only Suki found my dance funny.

Their parents came, they saw me as well, they screamed as well, the kids ran to them, and the next thing, they moved out of the house.

My worst mistake

Thinking that every kid will be like Suki was stupid. Suki was a special one and I realized that no one will probably replace her. And trying to make contact with those kids was the worst mistake I made as after this incident, the house has been probably declared as unfit for living or something. After this, nobody visited the house no more for a long time.

I was pretty sure that after a very very and very long time, eventually whatever happened will get forgotten and the humans will probably return. Until that, I have to be alone again. But how long its gonna take? I decided to myself that the only way for me to survive in this world is to be myself. No more Harry. I just have to forget that part of me. I must return to whom I was. To scaring humans. I'm not going to lose the next chance I get. So now, all I had to do is to wait. I have to wait probably for another two or three decades for the next set of people to come so that I can start my usual way of scaring them without revealing myself. But to my surprise, I had an unexpected visitor very sooner than I thought.

CHAPTER 7- WHICH PLANET?

After a year after the last family left the building, one night, I could hear strange noises coming from outside the house. I thought that the noise probably came from some sort of machine that the humans used to transport themselves from one place to another. All around the year, there wasn't even a single activity in or around the house. There was nobody except me. Why would someone decide to visit the area now? Maybe they have forgotten what happened in this house before? But ain't it too soon? Many questions rambled in my mind.

The noise kept getting louder, and the louder it got, the more I could sense that it was very different from the human-made machines. So, out of curiosity, I tried to peek out of the window to take a look at what it was. As soon as I peeked, I got burnt by a huge source of bright white light coming from some big object floating in the air. An object like which I've never seen before. I quickly hid back to relieve myself of the pain. What the hell could it be? I asked myself. The noise continued for a few more minutes and suddenly it all came to an end.

I peeked again as little as possible to see whether if the object was still there. But there was nothing. So, I thought, it was probably some humans who visited the place. I started to roam again. But throughout the night, I could sense that someone or something was moving here and there around the house. But I couldn't see what it was. I heard bushes outside rustling now and then, windows creaking, objects moving, doors opening, and several other noises around the house. But they were so mild that I wasn't sure if I actually heard something or if I was just imagining.

A visitor

I tried my best not to mind them. But the activities kept on increasing to a point that I simply couldn't help not to give attention to it. So, I started to follow the noises. I'm the scariest thing on this planet, what could be more dangerous or scarier than me? I asked myself, and to be honest I was a little scared. The fear of the unknown is indeed the greatest fear.

For several minutes, I couldn't find what was happening as the noises kept on coming from different places around the house time after time. Whatever made these noises could move very quickly. After a while, I gave up. I wasn't in the mood to search anymore. So, I went back to my doll and stayed in a corner doing nothing. I kept on hearing noises around until morning came.

And for the next whole day, until the sun went back to sleep, there were no signs of any kind of activity. I wondered what it must have been and wether will it happen again tonight. I was waiting for the day to turn into complete darkness. Finally, it became completely dark and I waited eagerly with my doll paying full attention. Suddenly, I heard a banging noise from the downstairs of the house. I kept the doll down safely and went down as quickly as possible to see what it was. As I went down, I could see that the wooden door was bust open as if someone or something busted it open to enter inside. While I was investigating it, I heard another noise from upstairs.

So, I went upstairs as quickly as I possibly could. I was shocked to see what happened upstairs. It was my doll. It was torn into pieces. The sight of it caused me immense pain. It was my only companion. It was the only thing close enough to Suki. I became furious. Whoever or whatever did this, must face my wrath. So, I went near a window and started to bang it as loud as possible to gain the attention of whatever that is moving inside the house.

I looked around while banging the window to see if I could spot something. At the end of the long hall, I could see a dark figure standing and staring towards me. From its shape, I was sure that it wasn't human. Neither it resembled any other living creatures on this planet that Suki showed me. It slowly started moving towards me. Whatever that was, it destroyed my doll. So my rage was still there. I banged the window even harder. I waited for it to come close enough to me so that I could unleash my terror.

Not this planet

It was a few feet away from me. But still, I could only see a silhouette of it due to the darkness. I widened my bloody eyes, opened my mouth of terror, and was ready to do my best to scare it. As it got much closer, I could see its features. It had three eyes on its forehead, one of which was a little bigger than the other two. The bigger eyes in the middle was completely dark, while the other two eyes looked like the night sky. Its body looked as if it was made of some kind of hard plastic. It came close enough to me and reached its long arms which had only one long and sharp finger.

Though its approach seemed friendly, my rage acted towards it differently. My instinct made me jump over it. I thought I would just pass through it. But instead, my body made contact. I felt strange when I grabbed its hand, I felt a strange kind of energy which I never felt before. As if I could do something to it. But it reacted back and threw me off. I was shocked that a living being could touch my body without any medium for the first time. Now, it was getting defensive and angry. It's bigger eyes changed its color to reddish-blue and it charged at me. I didn't back off either, I fought back. We fought for a while. We threw ourselves here and there over other objects around the house and even exchanged some punches and kicks. We could hurt each other physically. But our pain faded away quickly. Only if there was a human there, they would have seen probably the most epic fight on this planet.

We fought until the sun came up. I wasn't tired, but I could see that the strange being was tired. I had to stop anyway as I cannot resist the sun. So I stopped. The tired being slowly walked away somewhere. I went and hid myself away from the sunlight and was thinking all day about what just happened yesterday. But, there was a change in my mood. All my depression and loneliness seemed to be dulled after the fight I had yesterday. I felt really good and energetic.

CHAPTER 8- NEW COMPANION

I rested throughout the day. I gained my energy and was ready for another dual with the creature if it remained in the house after all the fight. Nobody can rule this house except me or of course humans. In other words, no other scary creature can exist in this house except me. So, I wanted to chase the thing away from the house. Night came and I waited to see or hear any signs of its presence. But there was only complete silence. I was losing my patience. I knew that it must be still hiding in this house. My senses were killing me. So, decided to find it. I searched here and there but couldn't find it anywhere.

The only two places that were remaining are the attic and the basement. I was pretty sure it wasn't in the attic as it must pass me to enter the attic. So, it must be in the basement and my guess wasn't wrong. It was indeed in the basement. It looked at me and simply stood there without attacking me. But I couldn't stay like it. I went towards it and started attacking. This time, it's attacks were a little bit defensive than offensive. So, I took advantage and started harming it very harshly. At a point it gave up and neither I felt like fighting anymore. It rested for a while and suddenly its bigger eyes turned into white. It started going around the basement picking up objects and showing it to me. Either it was showing off its collection or it was asking me what each object was. Either way, we didn't speak the same language so I didn't understand what it was trying to do.

After a while, I got bored of it and left it to be alone. I went back to my corner and started minding my own business. Days passed, and every day it goes out somewhere and returns before sunrise. Some days it just stayed in the house doing some noisy things. I never bothered it again. Time to time, I go down to the basement whenever it wasn't present in the house. The basement was its room and I was pretty sure that it was creating some weird technological stuffs for who knows why. But I didn't mind. After all, there was a comfort that someone was always home and I was not alone.

A strange device

One fine day, the strange thing visited me. It had some strange device on its hand. At first, I thought it was something it found in the house or somewhere outside. But it came closer to me, stared at me for a while. It slowly brought its pointy finger towards my forehead. I opened my teeth and was ready to attack. But it seemed calm and was not in an intention to attack me. So, I let it touch me as I was curious about what it wanted. After its hand made contact with my forehead, the device on its hand started making strange noises and my vision started to blur. I couldn't see or feel my body anymore. My vision became triple. I couldn't see the creature but I could hear it screaming from extreme pain.

Now I could see the place in which I was present a few seconds before, but I wasn't there. I was in the place where the creature was. And my vision was triple. My confused mind slowly started to realize. Whatever that technology was, it made me to get inside the creature's body. So, I tried raising my hand. But instead of my hand, I could see the sharp hand of the creature. Now I was sure that I was inside the creature's body. I tried to move around but it was difficult. I tripped and fell a few times but I was slowly getting a hold of it. It was quite exciting for me. But after a few seconds, I started to feel immense resistance. It was the conscience of the creature trying to resist. It dragged me towards the device which fell on the floor. I resisted as much as possible. But its conscience was stronger than me.

It was like its body has deducted my presence and it didn't want me in there. So, at a point, I gave up and let it go towards the device. It took the device and pressed some buttons. I could see different colors in front of me but I couldn't understand why. Suddenly, I was thrown out of its body and I could feel my own body and presence again. My sight became normal. But the creature seemed very weak after this event. It fell to the ground and screamed as it probably was suffering immense pain. Its eyes were flickering with various colors. After a few seconds, it took the device and crawled downstairs to its basement.

In the next few days, I did not hear or see it. So, I wondered what might have happened to it. I went to its room to check on it. It was lying in a corner and seemed to be sick. It knew that I was there, but it didn't mind me. I saw the strange device placed in a corner. I went towards it and tried to touch it. But the creature got angry and started attacking me. But as soon as I got away from the device, it left me. I understood that it didn't want me near that device and I could see that the creature was pretty weak as well. So, I didn't want to cause him harm anymore. After all, he was my only companion. I left him to rest.

But one thing was sure, when it comes to this planet, I was the evilest and powerful entity. I was sure after my encounter with such a strange being. But all those thoughts broke into pieces. A few days after I realized I'm not even close to the evilest thing on this planet.

Few months passed and the creature got its strength back again. It went on minding its own business of going out at dark times returning before sunrise. I was happy that he was back to form. But one fine day, I heard him screaming. I quickly rushed to check what happened. The creature was lying on the floor. There was a huge gap in its torso. Through the gap, I could see tiny, slimy balls with multiple colors oozing out. It immediately reminded me of human blood and I was pretty sure that it was badly hurt.

It was screaming for a while. I didn't know what to do. All I could do was bring a big piece of cloth and put it over its wound. It was pretty weak so I left it alone to rest. I don't how or what did this to it. Maybe it fell from a huge cliff, or, some beast could have attacked it, or even some humans could have attacked it. No, it probably wasn't humans. If it was a human, by now this place would have been filled with humans and their weapons. I felt sad about it.

CHAPTER 9- THE EVILEST

Few more days passed. Now and then I went down to check on its condition. I'm pretty sure it was healing but at a very slow rate. And it was still weak to even get up and do something active. One fine evening, I heard some noises down the floor. I was happy. I thought that the creature must have become healthy again. So, I went down to greet him. After all, we are brothers from different planets, or dimensions, or whatever. But as soon as I entered the basement, I found it still lying there weakly. Then what the hell made those noises. I heard some other noises again. It was as if someone was climbing upstairs.

I thought it might probably be some human. I was curious to see a human after all these years. As I reached upstairs, the noises continued to come from Suki's room. I was out of my mind. Could it be her? Could it be Suki? Did she come searching for me? I went near the room as quickly as possible and peeked. But it wasn't Suki. It was some other guy. In front of him on the floor, there was a woman. Her hands and legs were tied up. I didn't understand why, but the woman was unconscious. The guy looked around and slowly went down and out of the house. I hid in a corner and watched all these silently.

What the hell?

After a few minutes, the woman slowly became conscious. She looked around and clearly couldn't recognize where she was. Fear rose inside her and she tried to struggle and scream but she couldn't as she was tied up. I didn't know what to do. Should I try and scare her? But she was already terrified of something. Should I try and help her? But if I do so I will end up scaring her. So, I stood there watching that woman struggling helplessly.

After a few hours, it was midnight. I could hear someone climbing towards the room. I knew it must be the guy. So, I hid in the dark and watched patiently. As soon as the guy entered the room, the terror on the woman's eye instantly increased. She cried, pleaded, and did whatever she could. The guy didn't even open his mouth to say a word.

All these years, I have seen many humans. But this guy was one like I never seen before. His face had no expression. He came inside the room and brought along with him a heavy bag. He went out again and came back with another heavy bag. He opened those bags and turned the room into a different kind of set up. After a few minutes, he filled the room with sharp objects and weapons which the humans used to cut and kill things. He also had several other items such as ropes, candles, etc. Finally, he placed a huge image of a person who looked very calm and mesmerizing. The person on the photo seemed to be so pure and for some reason had wings and a ring over his head.

All the while when he did this, the girl kept on screaming and crying. The guy didn't even bother to look at her. He finished setting up the room and finally hanged the big image on the wall. He stared at the image for a while. He lit a few candles before the image, joined his hands, closed his eyes, and stayed still for a while. Then he opened his eyes and looked at the girl. He removed the tape from her mouth. The girl remained silent as she was shocked. He said "I want you to scream as much as you can while I do the necessary. I checked around and there is no human activity for several kilometers. So, go ahead"

What happened next shook me. I was petrified and speechless. The guy used every weapon in the room to slowly torture the woman, killing her minute by minute. I was pretty sure the woman had to go through immense pain that I could even possibly imagine. It took about an hour for him to do whatever he did. He made sure that the woman saw and experienced whatever he did to her. He inserted a device that kept her eyes open. So, the poor woman couldn't even close her eyes if she wanted to. And the scariest thing was that there wasn't a single expression or reaction on his face. He did all those things as if he was a machine. All those emotions which I saw amongst the humans, which made them stand unique from myself, were completely absent in him.

He did every torture possible and finally, when the woman was about to die, he took the burning candles that he placed in front of the image before and slowly burnt her eyes. The woman passed away. This was the first time I felt relieved that someone died. The guy was worse than all the humans I've seen before, even worse than the World war soldiers. Is he even a human? Or is he the evilest thing on this planet?

He then used a to tool and plucked those burnt eyes out of the woman and placed it in front of the image and again joined his hands and closed his eyes. After a few minutes, he took a big knife and started to cut her body into small parts and put it inside a bag. The blood was spattered all over the room. I took a look at the room and tried to imagine the days when I and Suki was in it and saw what it was now. Something changed in me. I just realized I'm not the evilest thing on this planet anymore. I became lifeless after seeing what just happened. It was a traumatic sight, even for me.

CHAPTER 10- HE KNOWS MY WEAKNESS!

Several days of horror continued. Almost every week the guy managed to capture and bring someone to the house. Many weeks he couldn't, but most of the weeks he succeeded. For a few weeks, I watched the horror that he did to those poor people. After that, it was too much for me. He always cut the victim's body into pieces and buried in the backyard. I couldn't even see the guy's face anymore. I just hid in my corner. I could hear the poor victims screaming with pain and agony. I'm nothing compared to this guy. I'm just an invisible being with a scary face that could scare weak hearted people, I thought.

The thing that bothered me the most was not the fact that I'm not the evilest thing on the planet anymore. But the fact that I couldn't do something about it nor, could I escape from this horror. I became dead inside. The screaming kept on continuing in my head even if there wasn't anyone in the room. I can't even peek into that room to get some memories of myself and Suki.

Poor thing

Amid all these terror, I completely forgot about my friend down in the basement. One fine day, I remembered it. But I was too broken to go down and check on it. Is it dead or alive? Is it even still in the basement or had it left me alone in this horror? Several questions in my mind. I heard the noise of someone climbing up the stairs.

I immediately knew it was the guy. He brought another victim and started his usual procedures. The screaming began and I prepared myself to go through the next few minutes of horror. In the middle of his ritual, I could hear someone else climbing up the stairs. I wondered who it was. To my surprise, it was my friend. The creature was attracted by all the screaming. It walked slowly as an ill person. I could see that it wasn't completely healed yet, but has recovered enough to walk and move. The creature noticed me immediately as I was hiding in my usual place.

The creature started to move towards the room. I tried my best to tell it not to go. I shook my head, hands, and whatnot. But it couldn't understand me. But then, I have fought with the creature. It seemed to be pretty strong than a human, especially with that sharp hands. So, I thought, maybe it could put an end to all this. If somebody can finish this guy, it should be my friend. I was nervous and was patiently watching what was about to happen. I prayed that my friend puts an end to that guy for everyone's good. The creature entered the room as I watched.

Even the creature was shocked by what was happening. But, surprisingly, the guy did not react to seeing the creature. He stood there with a sharp object drenched with blood on his hand. The creature stood there and was taking a moment to digest the horror. After a few seconds, the creature's center eye flickered with red and blue colors. Just like when it got angry and fought with me. That's my boy! Now go beat the shit out of him. I was saying to myself. The creature raised its hands, jumped over him trying to attack him. It caused some injuries, but the guy had two advantages. He had a hell a lot of weapons, which the poor creature couldn't grab it with its hands and the creature was weak.

I could see only one percent of the energy in the creature, compared to when it fought me. So, clearly, it couldn't show its full strength on the guy. The guy used the weapons to cause harm to the creature. Though the creature skin was pretty hard, it took some heavy damage which made it weaker. Yet the creature tried its best. But the guy was too smart and realized that the creature had a wound on its torso. So, he managed to pierce on its wound. The creature suffered from immense pain. It fell to the ground. I couldn't just hide and stand there watching my only friend die, I had to do something. The guy went and took a big and heavy sword from his weapon collection and raised it above his head to give a final attack that could potentially kill the creature.

I gained as much bravery as possible as my friend was about to die and I appeared before him quickly. I opened my mouth as wide as possible and tried to make myself the most scariest I've ever been. Again, the guy simply stood there still and watched me without any reaction. This bought some time for my friend and it slowly managed to crawl out of the room and downstairs to the basement, while I distracted him. The guy calmly walked towards the image, placed the sword before it, bent down, and started praying without minding me. His actions made me angry. What the hell is he doing there while I am here? I went near him when he suddenly took the sword and started swinging it all over me. This was the first time I was happy that I was incorporeal as the sword just passed through me. The guy stopped and thought for a minute.

He took the candles in front of the image and started bringing it towards me. The only thing that could hurt me was light. Now he found my weakness. Fear crawled back inside me. He slowly started walking towards me with the candle. The closer he got, the more I could feel the heat, and I started moving backward. His reaction-less face scared the hell out of me. So, I ran away from the room and hid as soon as possible. After a few minutes, I could hear the noises of him continuing his ritual. After this incident, I didn't even dare to move out of my hiding. His face was haunting me.

CHAPTER 11- THIS AIN'T HAPPENING

Two more weeks passed, and I had to go through another one of his rituals. I don't know what happened to my friend, but I wish it has escaped from this hell of a place. But after the last ritual, there wasn't another for a while. The guy came to the house now and then. He seemed to be pretty frustrated about something. Every time he comes without a victim, he goes directly to the room, stays there for a few minutes and leaves. I didn't know what he was doing.

One fine day, the guy entered again without a victim and went inside the room as usual. After a while, I could hear him screaming something. Out of curiosity, I went close to the room, to eavesdrop on him. He was screaming to the image, praying that he could find more victims as he was failing for the past few weeks to find one. The number of people missing because of him must have alerted the rest of them to be extra careful. So now, it has become much more difficult for him to find and lure a victim and he was pretty frustrated about it.

He was running here and there around the house screaming and yelling. He pushed down and broke various objects around the house. He cried, he laughed, he sat quiet, he cried again. He was mental. After a while, he just slept. That was the first night he slept in the house.

The next morning he just woke up and stayed still for a while staring at the wall. Then he went back inside the room and prayed in front of the image for a while. After that, he started to simply explore the house. He was going inside every room and every space around the house. I was just watching all his activities. He then went to the attic and was exploring there for a few minutes. But only then, the thought of my friend came to my mind. What if the creature was still in the basement? What if he wanted to check out the basement and found the creature? I didn't want to let this happen because I was pretty sure that, if the creature was still in the basement, it must probably be weak and resting from the previous injuries. So, I wanted to go to the basement and warn it if the creature was still there.

But I had one problem. Since it was morning, there was less dark places around for me to pass quickly. Either I have to go through the pain or not go. I chose to go, as I didn't want to lose my only friend. I went through immense pain to get to the basement and finally went inside. As I thought, the creature was still inside. But this time, it was only semi-conscious as its wound was pretty severe. It was very hard for me to watch it in such a condition. It couldn't even notice my presence. So, if the guy manages to find it, I was pretty sure that it would be the end of my friend. Who knows, maybe he may use my friend as his next victim. I thought a lot about what I could do to save him. No matter how much I thought I couldn't come up with a solid idea, especially with my incorporeal body. Every minute I could hear the guy moving here and there upstairs and I knew at any moment he could come down.

Finally, I came up with one final idea. Remember the creature's device which helped me to get inside its body during one of our previous encounters? What if I could use the device to enter inside its body and make it move to another place. But then, I also remembered how much the creature struggled with me being inside it, even when it was physically fit. So, in this condition, I feared I might end its life trying to help. While I was thinking about this, I could hear the guy climbing down the stairs. Now he was on the ground floor where the door to the basement was. I prayed that he entered some other room so that I could create some kind of distraction.

A brilliant move

I heard the screeching sound from the door of a room nearby. Now I knew that he was in the other room. So, I went out of the basement as quickly as possible and I could see the guy moving around in the room nearby. I planned to go back upstairs and create a distraction so that he forgets about the basement. But, there was one problem. The sunlight. Each time I pass through sunlight, my body gets caught in it and burns. Sunlight is like a magnet to my body. Once stuck inside, it becomes difficult for me to get out quickly. I went through immense pain again and finally managed to reach upstairs. But from there, I could see him moving out of the room and move towards the basement door. I used the available shadows and entered Suki's room as quickly as possible and pushed down the huge image to which the guy usually prays. The image fell to the floor and caused a huge noise.

There was silence for a few seconds. I quickly went back to my hiding and prayed that he shouldn't have seen the creature before he heard the noise. I heard footsteps climbing upstairs. It was him and he didn't look as if he noticed the creature. He sneakily walked upstairs and entered the room. After a while, I could hear him screaming "No..No!" as loud as he possibly could. I heard him cry for a while and I heard noises of the metals clanking. I went and peeked to know what was happening. I was really surprised to see what was happening. For whatever reason, after the huge image was broken, he must have thought that the place isn't suitable for him anymore. So, he started packing all of his weapons and put it back inside the bags.

He finished packing everything, took one last look at the room and took one of his heavy bags, and went outside. I couldn't believe it! I did it. Somehow I've put an end to all this. I was so excited. Now, everything can come back to normal. Now, my friend can heal peacefully back to health. The guy went out. There was only one bag remaining. Now all I had to do is to wait for the guy to come back and take his final bag and get the hell out of this house forever.

Pleasant and unpleasant

It was now evening and the sun almost went to sleep. I was waiting anxiously for the guy to return. Suddenly, I could hear footsteps. It must be him. A Few more minutes and he will take his final bag and disappear from me forever. I was thinking to myself. The footsteps got louder. I was excited to see the fool's face for one last time. But, I couldn't believe what I saw.

In the dark, a different human figure appeared. I'm sure it was not the guy as the human was a young female. The girl reached upstairs, stood there in the darkness, and was looking around as if she was searching for something. Then came a sweet sound from her mouth. "Harry? Are you still here? It's me.".

I was in ecstasy. I couldn't believe it! It was Suki! Is she real, or am I imagining? She looked and sound different now. But of course, I know that humans grow old. She moved further closer to me and that's when I jumped out of my hiding and appeared in front of her. Through the little light through the window, I was able to see her beautiful kind face. It was Suki indeed. She came back to me! My sudden appearance startled her a bit, but she recognized me. I never expected to see her again, ever in my life. After all the horror I have gone through, Suki was exactly what I needed to get my hopes back. Her pleasant voice gave me strength. Only if I could speak human's language and touch her I could express my true joy.

I could explain to her my stories of what happened all these days without her, she could tell me hers, and I could even introduce my new friend down in the basement to her. A normal human would fear my friend, but Suki was not a normal human. She would be happy to see my new friend for sure.

When I was thinking of my friend, all the memories of the horrors that happened before, suddenly came to my mind. The bag is still there, the guy hasn't left yet. The immense joy and excitement of seeing Suki after a long time, made me completely forget about the dangerous reality that was happening in the house. I saw immense happiness on Suki's face as well and she started talking to me. But unfortunately, there was no time for happiness. I have to get her out of this house immediately. So, I started using my body to convey the message that she must get out of the house immediately.

If anyone could understand my body language, it must be Suki. But as she lost touch with me for a long time she couldn't understand what I was trying to say. She was confused. But then, she came prepared. She took a doll out of her bag and handed it to me. That's my clever girl! I grabbed the doll and started to explain. That's when we both heard footsteps, climbing the stairs.

CHAPTER 12- DEATH

No, No, this shouldn't be happening. I said to myself. It was the guy. As soon as I saw his face I went into the hiding as I was scared. Poor Suki was confused about my sudden disappearance. She saw the guy and couldn't understand why he was there. A moment of silence existed between them. After a few seconds, Suki initiated the conversation. She inquired who he was and what was he doing here. The guy suddenly changed his reaction and acted like a normal person. I couldn't believe it if it was the same guy. He was so calming, lovely, and charming that even I started doubting how he could do such horrible things. Suki immediately fell for his acting and believed that he was a normal guy. He told her that he was just exploring the area, found the house, and then he decided to check it out.

Suki told him that she was a past owner of this house and that she just wanted to visit it for old time's sake. I knew what he is capable of and what his intention was. But I was so scared to even appear before him. After all, only I know that he is the most evilest thing on this planet. I was constantly thinking of what I could do to warn and alert Suki. They finished their conversation and Suki told him that she will be out in a minute after he saw the room in which she used to live. Please don't see that hell of a place, Suki. I thought to myself. Suki walked to what was once her room and was shocked to see what it has become. A room almost turned into red, by the blood splattering. It smelled like a thousand dead people. Suki immediately understood that something was not right. When she tried to walk away, the guy was waiting just behind her. Looking at her with his original reaction less face.

Suki knew he was dangerous and tried to do a surprise attack on his groin.

But the guy was a pro. He must have seen and faced hundreds of other girls like Suki and knew exactly how they will react. He anticipated her move and grabbed Suki's leg easily. He quickly twisted her ankle and displaced her leg making her unable to run away. She fell to the ground with immense pain. I couldn't keep hiding anymore. Especially not when Suki is in danger. I appeared in front of him and tried to distract him away. But he just stared at me with his dark, evil face. He didn't mind me, he knew that I was worthless. He just grabbed Suki's hair and started dragging her into the room. I followed them inside but didn't know what I could do. Only if I could touch him, I could have torn him apart by now. Suki tried to fight back, but the guy was too strong and hurt Suki badly. While holding Suki, who was struggling, with his one hand, he tried to reach his bag full of weapons with his other hand.

I knew that if he reaches the bag, that could be the end of Suki. But then, I realized that I could interact with the objects. So, I quickly tried to drag the bag away, but he managed to have a grip on it. I tried my best to pull it as hard as I can, but damn, he was extremely strong. He managed to slip his hand inside his bag while Suki was biting his legs as hard as she could. The guy didn't even flinch. He took a sword out the bag and that's when I heard Suki scream more and simultaneously I saw a sharp plastic-like object piercing and coming out of the guy's stomach. It was my friend. The creature somehow managed to climb up with the remaining strength it had and caused a heavy attack on the guy.

Suki was shocked to see a strange creature appearing out of nowhere and stabbing the guy. But the guy managed to take my friend's hand out of his torso, and give a strong blow at the creature's head. The creature fell to the ground motionless. That was the end of my friend. Though the injury caused by the creature was a severe one, it was just a flesh wound. The guy immediately removed his shirt and tied it around the wound to block the blood from leaking. While he was doing that, Suki quickly took her phone out and alerted the police and gave them her location. She tried to stand up but she couldn't move one of her legs. She tried to hop and drag herself, but by then, the guy caught her. I managed to take the bag with the rest of the weapons and throw it out of the window. But he still had one sword on his hand.

Suki warned him that she has alerted the police and that they could be here anytime. This made the guy angrier. He raised the sword high. I thought that was the end of Suki. But he gave a strong blow on Suki's head with the Sword's handle which knocked her unconscious. The guy didn't want to kill her like this. He wanted to perform his usual ritual, as finding another victim could be much harder if the police find that someone was murdered in the house. They could easily track him then.

So, he planned to take Suki away to some other place where he could perform his ritual. He hid the sword away and carried Suki in his soldiers and started climbing downstairs. Once if Suki was out of this house, there is nothing I could do to save her as I cannot even move an inch out of the house. So, I tried to do my best and pushed as many objects before him and on him. But he evaded them and walked through them without minding me. He reached the front door. I didn't know what to do.

This is how death feels like

I could see poor Suki's face hanging helplessly on his back. It felt as if my body was breaking into pieces. The guy hurt the only two living beings I knew and loved in front of me, and I couldn't do anything about it. Why was I created like this? What is the purpose of all these scary features that I have? I wished I could have never left the darkness and came into this world. I wished Sukran never brought me to this world. I felt how death must be even though I didn't die. Could I even die? No, I could only suffer until the end of time itself. Every day thinking about, how I stood there when that guy took Suki away. Thinking every moment of the cruel things that he will be doing to Suki. The amount of pain and suffering he is going to cause to Suki.

No, I can't let that happen, not to Suki. I rushed out of the house and tried to push myself as much as I could through the magical boundary which prevents me from getting anywhere from the house. The boundary pushed my body back and caused immense pain.

But I didn't mind. Either I somehow die or get out of this house and save Suki. I resisted the push for a while. I could see the guy moving with Suki, as fast as he could in a distance. But after a while, I couldn't resist anymore. I gave up and the magic threw me back inside the house. I was a failure. I'm nothing. I wish I could've been not me and someone else. I thought. But that same thought gave me an idea.

I quickly went down to the basement, took the device created by the creature, and hurried up near the creature's body. With the device on one of my hand's I took the creature's hand and placed it on my forehead. The device started making noises and bam! I was inside the creature's body. But this time, it was entirely different. Its body was 10 times heavier than last time and it was extremely weak. My friend was no more in there and I couldn't expect anything.

But, I was prepared to even die for Suki. So, trying to move around with a heavy body didn't stop me. It took a while for me to get a hold of it but I somehow managed. I fell several times, dragged, crawled, and finally got out of the house. I hoped this should work as this was my last chance before it becomes too late. I ran and jumped through the magic boundary. Though I could feel a push, the creature's body along with me inside, made it out of the boundary.

 Yes!, I did it! I started to walk as fast and possible and managed to even run for a while. But there was a problem. As soon as I came out of the magic boundary, I could feel something strange happening to my body. I felt like I was slowly burning inside an oven and I could even see steam coming out of the creature's body. But I didn't mind. My only goal now is to reach that son of a bitch and save Suki.

I started running as fast as I could. My body started to burn more and more. I could see beautiful mountains standing tall in the dark sky filled with stars, I could see the ground filled with different types of plants. Just as Suki described me, the world was truly a beautiful place. The humans are very lucky. But I had no time to cherish the beauty. I somehow managed to reach them. He immediately turned and noticed me. He placed Suki down and was looking for something to use as a weapon to attack me. By this time, I could not stand the burning, it was too much for me and the creature's body started to melt. I couldn't handle it anymore. It's not about my will power, but it was impossible. My body wasn't made to withstand this. Finally, I was going to die. I knew it. I got down to my knees. At least I tried Suki. I said to myself. I saw Suki there laying helplessly on the ground. The guy found a huge piece of rock and was moving towards me.

 I saw the guy's evil face and thought of all the cruel things he did. Then I saw Suki again. No, not after I came this far. I didn't come this far for nothing and I can't give up on Suki. So, I used whatever life left in me and jumped on the guy. The guy didn't anticipate my sudden action and I landed on him by inserting the creature's pointy claws inside each of his shoulders. He fell to the ground and I was above him with the creature hands stuck inside his shoulders. He was bleeding heavily and finally started to scream. He tried to move his arm and hit me with the rock, but I had no more energy to move. The burning got more intense and the creature's skin started boiling and melting as if plastic was melting.

It was as if hot melted plastic was poured over the guy's body. The guy slowly suffered and screamed as the creature's body melted over his body inch by inch, burning his skin, slowly killing him. I could finally see the terror on his face. I could see on his face, the same look his victims had on their face. Yes, who is evil now, my bitch? Well, thinking of what I have done, it's certainly not me, nor my melting dead friend. That's for sure.

Now the creature's body is completely melted and looked as if a bucket of black tar was poured over the guy. The guy got burnt by the melted creature's skin and died a slow and painful death. I was still trapped inside the melted body. The burning stopped and now I could see darkness starting to surround me. My vision was fading away slowly. I could see Suki moving there. She was gaining consciousness slowly. I could also hear police sirens nearby. My Vision almost faded completely. With the little vision left, I could see Suki open her eyes, turned her head, and looked at me for one last time.

Darkness surrounded me. I was back in this complete darkness. The place of nothingness, where I was before when Sukran found me. Nothing existed here except me. Not even time existed here. I was happy that Suki was fine. Even till today, I didn't know how was I born or who created me. Is there someone else like me?. I still didn't know what was my purpose during my time on earth. To scare every human was something that Sukran and the Witch made me believe was my purpose. If they hadn't said anything to me, I wouldn't have know what my purpose was. I said to myself, that I was the evilest creature on the planet. But Suki and the creature proved that I could be much more.

In the end, maybe life doesn't have a purpose at all. I could have existed simply without even doing anything. But we could create one by choosing whatever we feel like doing. We could either scare people or love and save people.

A long lonely time passed in this place of nothingness. And all I could think of was the moments with Suki and the moments that were created out of love. All the scary things I did never mattered for me. Suddenly, I saw a beam of light shining above me. There was a door-like opening. Just like when Sukran opened the door for me. I tried to watch through the light. I saw a strange head peeking through the door and there were three eyes on the head. It called me up.

....THE END...